My Family Is a Zoo

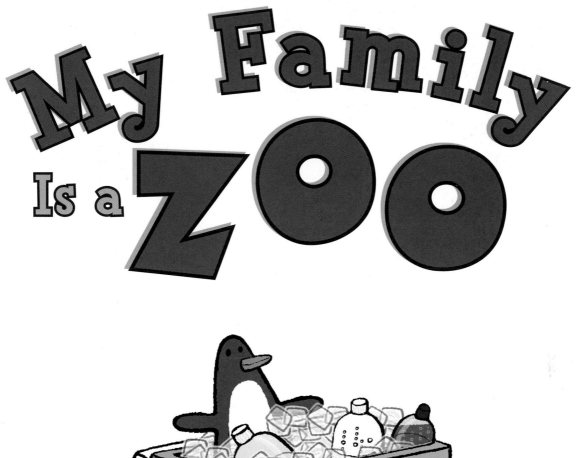

K. A. Gerrard   illustrated by Emma Dodd

BLOOMSBURY
NEW YORK LONDON OXFORD NEW DELHI SYDNEY

First published in the United States of America in March 2016 by Bloomsbury Children's Books
www.bloomsbury.com

Bloomsbury is a registered trademark of Bloomsbury Publishing Plc

For information about permission to reproduce selections from this book, write to
Permissions, Bloomsbury Children's Books, 1385 Broadway, New York, New York 10018
Bloomsbury books may be purchased for business or promotional use. For information on bulk purchases
please contact Macmillan Corporate and Premium Sales Department at specialmarkets@macmillan.com

Library of Congress Cataloging-in-Publication Data
Gerrard, K. A. (Kelly A.)
My family is a zoo / by K.A. Gerrard ; illustrated by Emma Dodd.
pages   cm
Summary: Everyone in my family has a special animal friend! My daddy has an elephant.
My grandma has a bunny. My cousin has a kangaroo. And me? I have a bear! Pile in with the
whole family—and more than a few of their favorite animals—for a special car ride.
ISBN 978-1-61963-851-8 (hardcover) • ISBN 978-1-61963-852-5 (e-book) • ISBN 978-1-61963-853-2 (e-PDF)
[1. Stories in rhyme. 2. Pets—Fiction. 3. Animals—Fiction. 4. Family life—Fiction.] I. Dodd, Emma, illustrator. II. Title.
PZ8.3.G3227My 2016   [E]—dc23   2015012105

Art created with pen and ink and Photoshop
Typeset in Amasis MT Std
Book design by Amanda Bartlett

Printed in China by Leo Paper Products, Heshan, Guangdong
1 3 5 7 9 10 8 6 4 2

All papers used by Bloomsbury Publishing, Inc., are natural, recyclable products
made from wood grown in well-managed forests. The manufacturing processes
conform to the environmental regulations of the country of origin.

For Emma, with love and gratitude
—K. A. G.

For Kelly, because you make me laugh,
and a day without laughter is a day wasted
—E. D.

My daddy has an elephant
He got when he was three.
It travels with us everywhere.
It's quite a sight to see!

Me, I have my big brown bear.
Surprise! His name is Teddy.
And whatever the adventure,
He is there, waiting and ready.

Today we're going for a drive,
To where I cannot say.

We should arrive by lunchtime
With some stops along the way.

Meet my sister and the whale
That she swims with in the ocean.
It's big and blue and blubbery
And smells of suntan lotion.

Here comes my older brother
With his purple dinosaur.
They may not *seem* ferocious,
But you should hear them **roar!**

Look! My cousin's kangaroo
Has a switch that makes it hop.
Perhaps the switch is broken . . .
The hopping just won't stop!

There's my uncle and his penguin
That he once left on the bus.
It traveled round for months
Before returning home to us.

My auntie owns a monkey
With sticky-outy ears.
She bought it on vacation.
She just loves her souvenirs!

Grandma's brought her bunny,
Whose coat is bald and worn.
It's been loved and hugged and cuddled
Since the day that she was born.

Grandpa's got his tiger
That once slept in their bed,

Till Grandma put her foot down.
Now it lives in Grandpa's shed.

Even Boomer has a puppy
That he carries in his jaws.
And every time he goes to sleep,
He hugs it with his paws.

Now we're all together,
With barely room to spare.
Can't wait to see if Mommy
Likes these brand-new polar bears.

We make a strange menagerie
As we pile out two by two.
We're not so much a family—
More a family zoo!

At last we have arrived—
Me, Ted, and all the others.
And just why have we come here?

To meet my baby brothers!